Dorm Daddy at Home

Dorm Daddy

AC Adams

Published by Wes Writers and Publishers, 2015.

Table of Contents

Dorm Daddy
At
Home
by
AC Adams

* * * * *

PUBLISHED BY:
Wes Writers & Publishers on Amazon
Dorm Daddy at Home
Copyright © 2014 by AC Adams

*****

****

Dorm Daddy

As it is with men's plans, they sometimes go awry. This was the case at local State University. Over the summer they had embarked on an ambitious building program that included new male dormitories. Come time for fall enrollment, the dorms weren't ready. To compound the problem, the minions at State had undertaken a huge freshman recruitment program that swelled the male freshmen enrollment beyond capacity. The new dorms wouldn't be ready until a month into the fall semester. The college put out frantic pleas to the community for help in housing its freshman males.

I ignored the pleas at first. Then the convergence of two circumstances forced my hand. The first was that I got laid off my job after being with those bastards for twenty years and literally sucking cock to reach the funky midlevel management position I held. The second circumstance was the frantic call from my friend Dean Wolf the Dean of Admissions at State.

"You've got to be out of your mind if you think I'm going to take any freshmen into my home. And what do I know about kids anyway?"

"You've got plenty of room in that big rambling shack. These aren't kids. They're young men, and you know a lot about young men. Plus, we're paying a generous weekly stipend of six hundred bucks per student," Dean Wolf wheezed and gasped into the phone. "And you don't have to feed them. Just house them. They'll take their meals at the University Cafeteria during the day."

He said two things that got my cock's attention right away, "money" and "men." And by the way he was gasping and choking on the phone, it sounded like he was wolfing on some guy's cock himself.

"Are you sick?" I asked. "Sounds like you're having an asthma attack, the way you're choking."

"Just come and fill out the paperwork tomorrow and we'll match you with one of the students—or two. And clean up that pigsty of yours. You'll have to buy or rent some bunk beds or twin beds. Students aren't allowed to share beds with each other ... or the resident." He was hinting at me of course.

"Two?" I asked.

He quickly hung up the phone without answering.

I arose early the next morning, and commenced to cleaning after I kicked out some rough trade who had spent the night. I wanted to make my home and my life spic and span for the innocent young freshmen. I gave extra attention to the spare room and bathroom next to my dearly departed Mom's room on the second floor. God rest her soul. She's been gone for six months now, but I keep her room like it was the day she left for the hospital. Her favorite red frilly negligee still lies across her four-poster Queen Ann Bed. Her room is a shrine.

I cleaned the spare room thoroughly, scraping dried cum from the walls and used condoms from the floor. Well, there had been a party last month and that's really all I'm going to say on that subject. I guess I could mention there were many twinkling brown eyes and long melancholy sighs of pleasure punctuated by my pal Brutus commanding us to either get on our knees or bend over. Every party needs a great host armed with a bamboo cane like Brutus. With the unpleasant task of scrubbing completed, I went to the army surplus store and rented two used military cots and two footlockers.

After the cots were delivered, I decided to chill and surf my favorite video site. I downloaded some videos from **18+HunkyDevils.com**. If I was going to have young freshmen in my home, I needed to know what I was in for.

In the video "*The Camping Trip,*" the Camp Master had a hard time keeping the gang of unruly young men focused on camp activities. They preferred staying in the bunkhouse sucking each other's cocks or carrying on with various mischievous acts in the shower stalls. Who knew boys could be so brutal snapping towels at each other's cocks and balls. I enjoyed the underwear raids where the older boys stole the newbies drawers and threw them in the river. Imagine the sight of twinks being forced to wear wet undies during camp inspections. Instead of using the latrines at night, they pissed outside their windows usually right into the face of the peeping tom Camp Master. They played games of who could make a cock come faster and shoot the farthest. Often the target was the poor Camp Master's face.

"Okay Ed, you know what you're in for," I said to myself as a watched the videos and stroked my cock. I found granddad's old leather belt and laid it across my favorite easy chair. I would tan some hides if need be, to keep order in my most humble domicile.

The next morning, I found myself face to face with Dean Wolf. Well, I sort of surprised him right in the middle of his favorite online video site, **SuckMonsterCocks.com**. He was licking the screen as a large cock pulsated and squirted loads of cum at the camera.

"Ahem!" I cleared my throat.

Dean Wolf nearly broke his neck whirling around in his chair.

"Can't you knock?"

"I did, but I guess you didn't hear me over the chorus of moans."

"We confiscated this from one of our students. I was checking to see if it violated school policy."

"A cock that size could violate your ass," I said.

Dean Wolf tossed a bunch of papers and a pen at me. After I filled out the paperwork that stated all of the terms and rules and regulations of the Temporary Auxiliary Housing Off Campus Agreement—The name was long enough to give me a headache—Dean Wolf walked me over to the gym where they were housing the freshmen males. I tried to excuse myself to use the toilet, but Wolf was not having that. He knows I have a bad habit of using the toilet in the men's dressing room for hours. I've visited him on campus before. It's always nice to see those bats swinging between thighs along with the plethora of bouncing balls. And of course, a cute melon-shaped ass, dripping wet, making it sweet and succulent to the tongue, is a nice treat. But Wolf wasn't allowing me to engage in any shenanigans today. I had to be professional and fatherly.

The young men were spread all over the gym floor. They each had a nice little sleeping bag. However, all of their belongings surrounded them as if they were refuges. Duffle bags, basketballs, blankets baseball caps, you name it. Some lounged sullenly on top of their sleeping bags with knees up and legs gapped listening to music on their iPods. Shorts tumbled down long legs, exposing pairs after pairs of black, bronze and white thighs. Silky blond hairs and curly black leg hairs covered the abundance of legs. I imagined my head buried deep in the darkness of those crotches. Some had taken off their shirts. A few gathered in shirtless clusters playing cards. I must have out-smiled a beauty queen. My jaws hurt. Much to my displeasure, they paid scant attention to me.

"I have in mind two very special candidates for you, Ed."

"Now wait a minute what's this two business? How do I know if I can handle one?"

"Two equals two six-hundred-dollar stipends. I'm sure twelve hundred boners, I mean dollars sounds nice to a man who's recently lost his job."

I shut up and let Wolf lead the way. Suddenly I was confronted with a huge rainbow banner hanging from the ceiling as if announcing a parade. I could actually hear the high-pitched voices of twinks before we even rounded the corner. I thought *Club Boyland* had invaded the place. Lady gaga competed with Beyonce and Nicki Minaj over peals of laughter and chattering voices. Like the straight boys, some of these "Friends of Dorothy" (Yes, I know that term is ancient history) also lounged with their knees up and legs apart. However, their eyes locked on us as if we were prey. They slowly opened and closed their legs as we passed, enticing us to fall into sinful traps.

"The Queen's Court," Wolf wheezed. God, my blood pressure rises every time I walk over to this section."

"I can see why," I said as I gazed at some cuties looking friendly and flirtatious. But one has to be cautious with young men. I've had many a twenty-dollar bill stolen from my wallet by flirty boys.

****

Just this past summer, I met a young man milling about the mall. I had ordered from McDonalds and sat down in the food court. He sat across from me and stared as I ate. I nodded at him, and he came and sat at my table. He said his name was Joel.

"I've been all over this mall looking for a summer job," Joel said. His eyes were sparkling pools of blue lust.

"Would you like for me to buy you a hamburger?" I offered.

"Oh yes, Sir. I haven't eaten since this morning. I spent all of my money putting gas in my mom's old car, so I could come to the mall and look for a job. I just graduated High school this past May. No one will hire me I guess because I just turned eighteen."

I looked into Joel's bright bluish puppy dog eyes and my heart just melted. I observed his thin frame and flat tummy as he retrieved the burgers and fries I had given him money to buy. His cute little butt poked out the back of his tight jeans in a nice way that reminded me of two ripe sweet grapefruits. I just imagined my tongue digging into that pink meat.

As we walked through the mall after eating, Joel stopped and looked forlorn at a pair of tennis shoes in a store window. We looked down at his dirty white sneakers. We left the store with a two-hundred-dollar pair of sneaks. Joel was very happy and hinted he would make me happy.

"I would love to follow you home and show my appreciation. Maybe I could mow your yard or something. I hope you have some wine, so that we can toast our new friendship."

"Now here's a boy who has some good character," I thought to myself. "And he's gorgeous."

He followed me home in his "Mother's" old black Impala. I stopped by the liquor store and bought a big bottle of red wine. There's nothing

like red wine to send red blood raging through a large cock. Joel and I
had two large goblets of wine as we sat and watched *Ru Paul's Drag Race*.
That's not my normal cup of tea. But whatever it took to float Joel's boat
and get him out of those jeans was fine by me. After the show went off,
Joel drained the last of his wine and licked his lips. He asked if I had
any chores for him to do, to show his appreciation. I pointed at the dirty
carpet and the closet where the vacuum cleaner seldom left. He sort of
pouted. I'm sure he expected me to point to the bedroom or his crotch
first. But I'm a practical guy. I wanted to get some kind of real work out
of him. It was his idea to come and show some "appreciation."

"It's so warm in here. You don't mind if I get comfortable, do you?"
Joel asked as he plugged in the vacuum.

"Of course not."

Joel stripped out of his jeans and polo shirt. His tight red boxers
hugged his ass so firmly images of succulent apples danced in my head.
My eyes followed his ass twisting as he pushed mom's heavy old iron
vacuum. His chest heaved as his muscled arms lifted chairs and tables out
of the way. What a worker, I thought to myself.

"You should get comfortable too," Joel said, when he was almost
finished.

By this time, I was draining the last drop of wine from the bottle. I
stood up and stripped out of everything but my t-shirt. I really should
work out soon, I thought to myself as I caught a glimpse of my big belly
in the mirror. Joel put away the vacuum and came and sat beside me. He
nuzzled his face into my hairy chest and lightly bit one of my nipples. I
yelped from the surprise, and he got up and ran out the door giggling.
I jumped up and chased him as he zigzagged all through the house. Just
when I thought I had him cornered, he'd leap over a chair and the chase
would be on again. I reached for his boxers but tore the elastic band.
You should have seen those torn boxers hanging off that cute jiggling ass.
I think he sensed I was almost out of breath. He let me catch him by
pretending to trip. My arms wrapped around his tight body.

I planted wet kisses on his lips and pink nipples. He lifted his hips for me to pull off what was left of his drawers. My tongue teased and trailed down his belly and flickered over his cock. Suddenly the whole thing was in my mouth down my throat. He moaned and arched his back. I sucked voraciously. When I felt the vessels in his cock stiffen like he was about to shoot, I let off. He tried to keep my mouth on his cock, but I had other things in mind. I lifted his legs and placed them over my manly shoulders. I put his balls I my mouth and nursed those two hard nuts like a chipmunk enjoying walnuts. I then licked the sweet spot between his balls and ass. I went further down. His cute barely hairy pink asshole winked at me. I plunged my tongue deep inside. He arched his back and acted as if he was going to pull my head inside of him. I let my tongue flicker over the pink hole then plunge in deep. This went on for what seemed like hours. He grabbed his dick and began to jerk and moan. I grabbed mine. After a moment we exploded in white rain all over our bodies. We lifted ourselves off the floor and stumbled to my bedroom. I was soon in a state of dreamland.

When I woke up the house was dark. It took me a moment to figure out why I was naked. I reached over and touched air. I sat up and yelled out, "Joel!" There was no answer. When I found the light switch, the blaring light shined on the empty table where the TV had sat. Drawers were rifled and my things spilled out all over the floor. When I checked my wallet, it was empty. In the driveway sat his "Mothers" old Chevy and gone was my new Dodge truck. The cops told me I had been taken by a member of the "*Goodboys Gang*." They work the malls in various cities cuckolding older dudes with their manners, good looks, and sad stories. It turned out that Joel's Mom's car was a stolen vehicle. He was probably on his way to Dallas or beyond to entice another victim.

****

As Dean Wolf and I walked under the rainbow banner, two young men were suddenly engaged in a loud argument. They got right each other's face and pushed one another until Wolf got in the middle of them. They were gorgeous and slender. One was the color of honey and the other was a nearly bronze. Wolf whispered that one was half white and half black and the other was Puerto Rican and half Asian. Dark curls ringed their foreheads and they were almost the same height of 5'10". Their full pouty lips were inches apart before Wolf separated them.

"Meet Juan and Aaron," Wolf said smiling a little sheepish as if he had known them in an intimate and private way. I took Wolf aside.

"I won't have two fighting twinks disturbing the sanctity of mom's house."

Wolf looked at me queerly. "Ed, the old hag's been gone six months now. Are you okay?"

Wolf could get away with calling Mom an old hag. They were cousins several times removed.

"Yes, but..."

"But nothing. Two fighting cocks is just what you need to help you get over your grief. They're actually very good friends."

Wolf explained they were both from New York, but one was from the Bronx and the Other Harlem. "They're just having a bit of homesickness."

Wolf led me back to the boys and we sat down at a table to get to know each other. It was hard to resist those beaming smiles. Long gone was the snarling and shouting. They oozed manners and politeness as I asked questions. Those beautiful pearly white teeth gleamed as we chatted. I decided to give them a chance after Wolf said they had been straight-A students at their former High School.

They gathered their belongings on an overflowing hotel luggage cart and pushed it out to my car. Other boys looked at me sadly as if the say, "Take me, Daddy." And at that moment I wish I could have taken them all.

"I thought you were going to have a cool car like a Porsche or a "Vette." Juan looked disappointed at my little blue Corolla.

"Yeah," Aaron chimed in. "Most older guys have hot cars for their boyfriends to drive."

"You gentlemen are not my boyfriends. I should have brought a U-Haul for all of this crap you're cramming into the trunk and back seat."

"We had to live in a U-Haul for a day. That shit ain't cute," Aaron said as he pulled his duffle bag from the cart. It was so heavy it swung him around and he bashed into the Corolla's back door. I held my breath at the sight of the small spoon-sized dent. After we loaded the car, another tiff broke out. They argued over who was going to sit next to me.

"Are you guys nineteen or nine," I asked. They pouted like two nine-year-olds. Lucky my car has a center console that folds up and turns the bucket seats into one long bench seat. Aaron slid next to me, and Juan sat next to the door with his elbow out the window.

THE RIDE HOME

I expected the ride home to be a nice pleasant one with talk about their plans for college. Instead, they sat and elbowed each other.

"Who has the biggest cock," Juan asked and giggled.

"My dick is bigger than both of you guys put together," Aaron said proudly.

"Braggart," Juan huffed.

To my utter shock, both boys pulled their cocks out and started comparing them in the front seat. My car is small and with all their gear loaded it was very low to the ground. I'm sure folks in trucks and big SUVs had a clear view of everything going on.

"Put those things back in your pants right now!" I smacked each of their cocks and they seemed more tickled than in pain. They giggled and began smacking each other's cocks. "Stop that now," I yelled. But I'm sure I sounded more like an old granny than some in-charge man. Speaking of the elderly, what happened next literally gave me a heart attack.

"Look, there's an old lady at the bus stop ahead." Juan shouted.

"Wow! Let's give her a nice big smile," Aaron laughed. And before I could say Moon over Miami, both boys had undone their seatbelts and rolled down the window. They pulled down their shorts and stuck their cute little asses out the window. Aaron reached over and honked my horn just as I passed the surprised woman. In the rearview mirror, I saw her staring at my car with the look of utter shock on her face. By the time I could say anything, they had scooted back into their seats.

"Do not ever do that again," I screamed.

"We won't. We only do it once a day." Juan chuckled.

"It's better than getting high," Aaron added.

"You boys seem to be really good friends," I said after I calmed down. I wanted to keep their minds off of any more mischief. Though they were from different boroughs in New York, they had gone to the same high school, Gifted Arts Academy for Boys, I remembered Dean Wolf saying.

"Gaaahhhh!" Aaron shouted.

"Gaaaagggg!" Juan shouted back. He stuck two fingers in his mouth to indicate sucking a cock.

"Gifted arts, you trained our cocks to conquer the world," they sang in unison. If that was the school song, I wondered what went on in those hallowed halls.

"How come you haven't shown us your cock?" Juan asked peering around Aaron and looking intently at me.

"Yeah," Aaron agreed. "You've seen our dicks, but you haven't shown us yours." Aaron reached over and touched my crotch. I slapped his hand away.

"Gentlemen, I will do no such thing in this car."

"You'll show it to us when we get to your house?" Juan asked.

"Absolutely not."

"Aww, you're no fun," Juan whined.

"I thought when the Dean said he was letting us stay with someone gay, he meant cool like us." Aaron pouted.

"And cute like us," Juan added.

"Are you one of those older guys with a cute young boyfriend we can fuck while you're at work?"

"I think you and Freckles will get along just fine."

"That sounds like a dog. Eeww bestiality!" Juan screwed up his face.

"Freckles is a cat," I said.

"Bitch, shut up. You'll let anything with a big dick up into that boy cootchie of yours." Aaron teased Juan.

"And who sucked everybody's cock on the Soccer team?"

"You young men are trying my nerves. I think we should stop and get pizza."

"Yeah, maybe we can get a hot delivery boy in the bathroom stall."

"I think it's going to be pizza to go," I said.

"We want cum toppings," They screamed and giggled.

Thank goodness we were able to leave the pizza parlor without any major embarrassments. Although Juan and Aaron did spend a wee bit too much time in the restroom after a cute Ethiopian delivery boy went inside. I grew concerned and went to investigate. I saw three pairs of tennis shoes in one stall and two pairs of pants draped over ankles.

"Gentlemen!" I yelled out, only to be greeted by grunts and a toilet flushing.

"Nothing like a free pizza," Juan said slamming the car door and sitting the extra large on his lap.

"Yeah. If Wilbur here had stayed out of our business a little longer, we would have gotten free sodas too."

"Ed," I corrected him.

As I drove off, I saw the cute Ethiopian pizza guy standing by his car zipping up his fly. I started to ask what had gone on in that restroom stall but decided I'd better not. Still, I would have like to have seen his cock. The next time I order pizza in, I'll ask for the Ethiopian delivery boy.

"Show us the cruisy areas," Juan shouted.

"Yeah, show us where the rent boys hang out. I want to see some dicks."

"Didn't you guys have enough fun in the pizza place?"

"Is there an expiration date on fun?" Juan looked at me.

"Maybe there is. You see how old Wilbur is," Aaron snickered.

"Ed!"

Just to placate the boys, I drove around the area near the Greyhound Bus Station. The streets were narrow, and the landscape dotted with abandoned stores, a couple of homeless shelters and a tree whose trunk someone decided to decorate with used condoms. I'd love to meet that artist. I hope he wears rubber gloves on his hands and wherever else. Being in the middle of the day on a Friday afternoon, there were a few specimens out besides the normal crack scarred regulars. A few hustlers were dressed preppy as if they had slipped away from the nearby

Community College. As I cruised by a few pulled out their beautiful black cocks from their open flies and shook them at the car.

"Wow look at that bratwurst. Pull over, Wilbur so I can get a feel."

"Boys he may be a cop."

"If he is, I'm going to jail right now as long as he handcuffs my ass to that dick."

I pulled over and the boy seemed friendly and eager to approach the car. He could tell by those two ravenous pups with their tongues hanging the window, we weren't undercover cops. He leaned into the car.

"Sup, niggas?" His voice was a deep bass fiddle. Juan and Aaron swooned and cooed. Even I felt the heat rush over me. It was September but felt hotter than July. His dark brown dick snaked out of his pants and halfway down his thighs. Veins crisscrossed from the red tip and got lost in the nest of pubic hair.

"Hey man, can we get a feel?" Aaron looked up with brown puppy dog eyes at the young hustler. The boy stood up and stretched so that his cock leaned over the window and into the car. Aaron and Juan stroked and caressed the cock until it started to rise and stand at attention. They began to lick at the tip and got as far down the shaft as the partially opened window would allow.

"Let down the window, Wilbur," Aaron screeched. "We want more of that dick."

I guess I was sort of irritated by being called Wilbur and I was worried about cops. I hit the window switch, but instead of the window sliding down, it went up and clamped on the cock.

"Yow! Mother Fucker!" The hustler screamed out in pain. I panicked and fumbled more buttons. The back windows opened and closed, and the doors unlocked and locked. It was lucky that Juan was sitting by the window and hit the roll-down switch enough for the boy to free his cock. I sped off. In the rearview mirror I saw a cop car approaching the hustler who stood bent over massaging his dick.

"What a dork," Aaron hissed at me.

"Is this one of those moments we are going to look back at and fondly remember?" Juan asked.

I smiled to myself. It was certainly something I was going to remember when I jacked my dick tonight.

Home

"Wow what a big old house," Juan said. "This looks like something out of *Psycho*. Do you have a playroom in the basement?"

"This is Houston. Houses here don't have basements," I said.

"Where do you keep your sling? Do you have a playroom?"

"This is a respectable house, not some tawdry spa or men's club."

"It's a big ass house. Man, we need to have an orgy in here."

"Well first you better learn where your room is and where the bathroom is." I led the boys upstairs. They crept along as if they were in a haunted house. All I needed was Dear Ol' Mom to appear out of nowhere dressed in one of her naughty nighties.

"Who's the old lady in the shorty nightgowns?" Juan asked as we passed the large, framed photos of Mother posing in her negligees.

"My Dear departed Mom," I sniffed.

"Wow, your mom was a freak," Aaron said.

"She had been a lingerie model in her younger years," I beamed proudly.

"She didn't know when to stop," Juan said under his breath. I ignored him and pointed out their room.

"Ooh, military style bunks. I like that. But how come we don't have a TV?"

"The agreement doesn't call for TV in your room. You can watch the tube in the living room."

"This bitch better have cable and wifi or I'm bailing." Juan said.

"I have all of the modern conveniences," I huffed.

"I was just saying..."

Suddenly Freckles appeared to greet the visitors.

"Holy shit! Is that a fucking leopard?" Aaron screamed.

"Just an ordinary house cat. The only thing he cares about is his tail and his next meal."

"Our neighbors had cats," Juan said. "But they'd cook 'em and eat 'em. They were Chinese or some kind of Asians."

I scooped Freckles up in my arms and showed the boys their bathroom so they could wash up for supper. I went to the kitchen set out plates for our pizza. They came downstairs dressed in their skimpy boxers.

"I don't think that's dinner attire." I stood pointing at their near nakedness.

"This is how dudes dress in a dorm, pops."

"Ed!" I corrected.

"Yeah, it sure is," Juan agreed. "Right before I graduated, I visited a Senior at NYU. All the dudes hung out in their draws, unless they were going to class."

"How many cocks did you suck that day?" Aaron asked.

"I don't know man, fitty maybe?" They laughed and high-fived each other.

"How is your pizza," I asked trying to steer the conversation away from cocks.

"Good. I can put the whole slice in my mouth without gagging." Aaron chuckled at Juan and tried to imitate him. He wound up spitting out half his pizza. After they ate they bounced to the living room and sprawled on the couch.

"Wow what's this box do," Juan asked looking at my big tube-in-the-back flat TV.

"It's a television."

"Looks like it only plays old school TV like Lucille Ball."

"Or Maverick. You look like the kind of dude who would like Maverick. That was my Granny's favorite show. I think she died masturbating to Maverick."

"My Granny was a dyke," Aaron said.

"Boys! That's enough about your family tree. Let's watch TV."

"Who's that little girl with the curly hair," Juan pointed at the large gold framed photo resting atop the television."

"That's me when I was five. Mother kept me in dresses and little nightgowns until I had to start school." I beamed proudly at the memory.

"Wow," Juan said with a worried look on his face.

"I have to shit out some of this pizza," Aaron said and skipped toward the hall bath. Juan jumped up and trotted behind him. I had no idea taking a shit was a community effort.

"Come see, Wilbur!" Juan shouted.

"Ed!"

When I got to the door Aaron was sitting on the porcelain throne butt naked of course. His boxers were on the floor in front of him. He looked like he was trying to have a baby from his ass.

"Oh girl, you look like you're taking three cocks at once."

"Can you close the door?" I shouted and fanned my nose.

Juan stepped in the bathroom and closed the door behind him. I wondered how he was able to stand the smell, but I didn't say a word. I was glad they were out of sight and out of mind for a minute. I dozed on the couch as Bruno Mars crooned in his latest video about making love like gorilla. Just the right kind of song for the two monkeys in my house.

A moment later I felt water sprinkling my face. "Ah the favorite part of my dream," I thought to myself. The entire boy group Menudo and I splashed in waves along a secluded beach. They reached into the water and slipped off their swim trunks and threw them high in the air. I always woke up as the brightly colored trunks fell gently toward my upturned face. I've been having this dream on and off for twenty years. I think Menudo may be grandpas now. My eyes barely opened. Juan and Aaron stood in front of me butt naked and dripping wet. I thought I was still dreaming as one coco brown body and one caramel colored body weaved in and out of my dream state. Both stomachs flat, nice boyish muscular thighs. And you can just imagine my mouth parting at those two beautiful cocks. Aaron's was dark brown and hung to the left with a slight curve upward. It had to be at least ten inches. Juan's was dark pink and as fat as a juicy cucumber. Neither young man was hard. In my dream state, I reached for those cocks.

"Hey man!"

My eyes popped open.

"There's no towels for us to dry off with."

I got up and gave them two big fluffy towels each. They promptly wrapped them around their waist and rejoined me on the couch.

"What kind of porn you got around here, Daddy Ed?"

"I don't think you're allowed to watch porn in your dorm. The rules strictly state I'm to follow the same rules in my home as you would experience in a dorm setting."

"Aww don't be so uptight. This haunted house is nothing like a dorm. The toilet flushed by itself while ago."

"Yeah man. You don't have to follow those stupid rules from Dean Wolf. You still haven't shown us your cock."

"And I don't intend to."

"You've got nice arms. Very muscular." Aaron stroked my arm.

"Thank you."

"And nice thighs." Juan stroked my thighs. I reached to remove his hand. Suddenly Aaron started tickling me furiously. Hands were all over me tickling my sides and nipples. I'd try to reach up and control one pair of hands and another would take over. I felt hands tugging at my shirt and felt it being yanked over my head. More tickling continued all over my tummy and nipples. I laughed so hard, I sounded like a mule hee-hawing. Juan straddled me while Aaron unbuckled my trousers and pulled them off along with my undies in one swift motion. Juan didn't let up tickling.

"Say Uncle, Ed. Say Uncle or we won't stop." They both continued from my nipples to the bottom of my feet.

"Uncle!" I cried out. I could stand no more. Juan and Aaron rolled off of me.

"Wow!" They screamed. They took turns holding my eleven-inch cock and big balls. "Shame on you for hiding these treats from us." Juan slapped my balls. I yelped.

"Get to work, Pizza girl," Aaron said.

Juan bent over and started licking my semi-hard cock. He started lightly flicking his tongue over and around the head. My cock pulsed and blood stretched it hard and tight. He worked it little by little into his mouth. In the meantime, Aaron was working his soft plumb lips over my nipples and neck. He worked his way down my belly and joined Juan at my cock. He licked the base while Juan continued working the monster into his mouth. Aaron then continued on to my balls and worked one ball at a time with his tongue.

My eyes rolled in the back of my head. My muscular man thighs were pulled wide apart. Aaron left my balls and traveled farther down south. They pushed my knees closer to my body so that my ass hole was more exposed. Aaron flickered his tongue lightly over my hole. He then pushed it in and pulled out like he was tongue fucking me. I was driven mad with ecstasy. I began to whimper as my body quivered. My breathing became shallow.

"Let's watch him shoot," Aaron whispered to Juan.

Juan let off my cock. I grabbed and jerked it about four times, before I began to bellow like a bull. The boys leaned over me. Their faces close together. My load shot out and hit their cheeks, lips, and eyebrows. They squealed in delight and licked each other's faces greedily. They then jacked their cocks in my face, and I was slathered in boy lotion, which they promptly licked off. We fell asleep in a pile on the couch.

****

It's been a couple of weeks now, and I must admit it's a nice sight seeing two half naked young men parading around the house and lounging on the couch with their slender thighs up and boxers bunched at their crotches while they watch TV or do their homework. Sometimes they traipse through the house in their little bikini briefs.

I try to be as modest as I can around the young men. But they seem to enjoy bursting in the bathroom while I'm taking shower. As I'm drying off they sit on the toilet giggling and trying to grab my cock. Of course, I chase them out and the next thing you know I'm running through my house butt naked chasing two round butts with a belt in my hand.

I have to supervise them like young boys. They even fight over who is going to use the toilet first. You should see them butt naked trying to elbow each other off the commode. There's nothing like seeing a cutie sitting on the toilet eating an apple as they go. They always seem to leave a nice little turd for daddy to flush away. Thank God they piss standing up. That's a nice sight. I love seeing and hearing piss gush from those two large cocks at the same time. But did they have to do the piss fight? Yes, a piss fight. Lucky, I don't have rugs in their bathroom. I passed by the bathroom door one day and they're aiming their cocks at each other like water pistols and squirting each other with piss. When I tried to stop them, they promptly shot a blast right into my yelling mouth. Oh, where do boys get their habits? "I'm fit to be tied." Mom would say.

One thing is I'm grateful of is that they don't mind being in the restroom together and even being in the shower at the same time. It saves a lot on the water bill. There's a very clear shower door in their restroom. It's nice seeing two pairs of soapy bronze buns bouncing and jiggling as they shower. I love to see them applying lotion to their backs. Or better yet, I like it when they ask me to do the honors. My hands always stray too far. I wind up applying lotion to a pair of wet buns or giving them both hard slaps that sends them yelping down the hall.

Now State University had said nothing about freshmen weekend activities, except that they be wholesome and charitable—whatever that means. So on the weekends the boys like to go to *Club Boyland*. One rule I set was that they could not use my car. And no amount of begging and teasing could make me budge.

That meant I had to drive them to *Club Boyland* the favorite hangout spot for young men between the ages of 18 and 24. How cute they looked sprinting around in their undies trying on all sorts of combinations of tight jeans and tight shirts. They slathered themselves with lotions and body creams as they got ready for the night.

"Wow, we look like a couple of dorks being dropped off by Daddy," Juan complained as we drove up to *Club Boyland*.

"You could have caught the bus," I said.

"Are you kidding us?" Aaron looked incredulous.

"What time do you want me to pick you up?"

"Thanks, but we'll find rides back home," they said as they bounced from the car.

Ah, *Club Boyland*. I remember my times going there as a younger man. I'd walk in with one boyfriend, break up with him and leave with a new one. I remembered all the cocks I used to suck behind the closed stalls. Well, what is there to do now except go home and curl up with a movie and a bag of popcorn with Freckles lying across my feet. Which is exactly what I did. In less than an hour, I was fast asleep.

I was awakened by soft tiptoes in the living room and low voices. "Well, I guess those two urchins did get a ride home," I said to myself and prepared to roll over and catch more Z's. But then I heard other unfamiliar voices and giggles. I got up and tipped to my door and cracked it a bit. Two tall handsome boys, one white and one black walked out of the hall bathroom toward the living room. Beautiful cocks side to side like pendulums.

"Hurry up, niggas!" Juan and Aaron hissed.

"Chill out, niggas. We had a lot of drinks we had to piss out. Them assholes better be lubed."

"They ready for them dicks," I heard Aaron whisper.

The boys turned toward the living room instead of Aaron's and Juan's room upstairs. I guess they didn't want the noise of all of that fucking above my head to wake me up. They make enough noise causing those bunks to squeak with all of that jacking late at night.

I tipped out of my bedroom and glided down the hall. I peered around the corner and there were those two gorgeous hotties standing over Aaron and Juan.

"What a creepy house you dudes stay at," I heard the black boy say as he looked around.

"Yeah man, looks like it ought to be dead bodies lying around. Who's the old broad in all of these pictures?" The white boy asked.

"It's just Wilbur's dead Mother," Juan answered as he reached for his buddy's cock.

Ed! I wanted to scream out. I'm not sure why those two morons slip and call me Wilbur.

"Wow! She must have been some kind of old Playboy bunny or something the way she's wearing all them negligees."

"I think she was some kind of perv. She made Wilbur wear dresses," Aaron said.

"Wow I hope we never meet that dude."

"If you two don't shut up about this place, we're going to put our cocks in your mouths," Juan hissed.

I soon heard moans and groans. Aaron and Juan sucked those cocks like they were the last dicks on earth. Spit dribbled down their chins. I never knew jaws could stretch so wide and make a cock disappear. The guests pulled their cocks out and beat Aaron and Juan on their lips. "Suck them dicks! Suck them dicks!" That energized Aaron and Juan even more. They dived right back in.

The sucking was just a little appetizer that lasted a few moments. After that, legs went up in the air, lube got squirted into assholes, condoms got rolled on and they were off to the races. Aaron had one leg locked around Juan's thigh as the white dude plowed into him. Juan played with his black friend's balls sending what must have been electrical charges to his dick. The boy pumped furiously. It was a sight to behold—a beautiful black ass working hard pushing that black dick all up in Juan's gaping asshole. Juan reached around and slapped the boy's ass hard as one might slap the flanks of a horse to make him work harder. Aaron's white hottie plowed into him equally as hard. Ass cheeks flaring open to expose a sweet brown eye for the world to see. I had to grab my own cock and jack as I watched them having a ball on my poor dear departed Mother's couch. Juan's boy lifted his ass higher and plowed deeper. I listened to that "shlock shlock" sound and farts sputtering as asses got plowed deep. Balls slammed like bags of hard nuts against bottoms. Aaron and Juan jacked their dicks and kissed each other as they were getting fucked.

Soon the white boy began to bray like a mule. "Shhh," Juan whispered. But he couldn't stop himself from groaning loudly. The room erupted into an orgasmic chorus of grunts, ooh and ahs. I hurried back to my bedroom and had a nice little eruption behind my closed door.

****

Now being the sly cuties they were, Juan and Aaron soon had me breaking the rule about not driving my car. What can you say to a couple of young men standing in a pair of cute jockstraps right beside your bed?

"Hey Ed, what are you doing?"

"I believe I was taking a nap," I said irritably before I opened my eyes. I popped one eye open. Nothing is more exciting than seeing cute young men in jocks. I envy college coaches being in the midst of all of those tight buns. Before I knew what was happening, Aaron leaped in my bed and straddled my body. Juan pulled the sheet down. And there I was stark naked.

"You need a massage," Aaron said. He commenced to massaging my chest and nipples. Juan rubbed my thighs and inner thighs. He lifted my legs and worked my cock and balls with warm oil. They watched me like a pair of kittens as I moaned and writhed.

"How does that feel, Daddy?" They crooned in unison.

All I could do was go, "ahhhhhhh" as their wicked fingers lightly pinched my nipples and gently squeezed my balls. Juan grabbed my cock and tickled Aaron's ass with it. In fact the light brushing of Aaron's ass was giving my cock heavenly fits. And of course, it didn't help matters that he was squeezing and massaging it too.

"Ed, do you like us," Juan asked.

"Of course, boys," I managed to gasp between breaths.

"Will you do us a favor?"

"What?"

Juan slapped my cock between Aaron's ass cheeks. He and I both yelped in pleasure. "Just say yes," He pleaded with me.

"Yes, Yes Yes!" I crowed as I was about to come. Juan let up squeezing my cock.

"Can we borrow the car tonight?" Juan sensed my hesitation and applied more pressure to my balls. He brushed my cock against Aaron's ass. I began to moan.

"Please, daddy," Aaron whispered and bent down and gently nibbled my nipples.

"Yes! Yes! Yes! Just let me come! Please!"

"Okay daddy, you promised." With that Juan released my cock. I grabbed it and began jacking it like mad. Soon I had sprayed both boys with a healthy dose of man juice. They licked it off themselves, kissed me, and started planning their wardrobe for the evening.

"Cuckolded again," I thought to myself. But what can one say to two cuties giving such thorough massages?

****

It was Sunday morning and I went out to inspect my car. Juan and Aaron had come home alone. I checked on them as they snoozed totally naked in their bunks. To my surprise there was a scratch on my little ol' Toyota that I kept in immaculate condition. I was livid with anger. However, I let them sleep while I thought about how I would punish them. They woke up around noon and slouched into the living room without a stitch on.

"Put on some pants," I commanded.

"Why? We're not going nowhere," Aaron said sullenly.

"Put on some pants, both of you. I want to know what happened to my car."

The boys tugged their jeans on, and we all marched outside. They stood around the car looking at it foolishly as if they didn't know what it was.

"That scratch right there," I yelled to get their attention.

"Oh wow," they said.

"Who was driving?" I asked.

They pointed at each other.

"You both weren't driving at the same time," I yelled.

"We don't know how the scratch got there. It might have been Freckles."

"Cats don't scratch cars."

"Cats do strange things," Aaron commented.

"Well, I'm going to do some strange thing to your asses. Get back in the house."

"What are you going to do to us?" Juan whined with a worried look on his face. Juan and Aaron marched just ahead of me back into the house. I went and grabbed one of my old belts out of the closet.

"Turn around and pull those britches down," I demanded as I came back into the dining room.

They both turned and unsnapped the top button of their jeans.

"Down I said."

They gave a little tug and those jeans slid over those two pairs of sweet cakes.

"Step out of them."

"You can't do this to us," Juan cried. "We're college boys."

"Shut up! Or no more car privileges."

They both held each other and stepped out of their jeans. They looked over their shoulders at me holding the belt.

"Bend and grab your knees and spread your feet apart!"

They did as I told them. Just imagine, two perfectly shaped round asses at your mercy. I wrapped the belt over my hand and snapped it across Juan's ass cheeks first. I used light strokes just hard enough to make their asses quiver and sting but leaving no bruises. What a sight watching those cocks and balls bouncing between those legs and those hands grabbing their ass cheeks as if they were trying to put out a fire. Finally, I figured it was enough cheek spanking. It was time for round two. I went to Mother's old chest of drawers and found two pairs of her pinkest panties and made Juan and Aaron put them on.

"Now go stand in the corner," I commanded. After thirty minutes of them standing and scratching their asses, it was time for round three. I drove the car onto the patio behind the house. I ran a tub of nice sudsy water and picked out two nice brushes.

"Come on, boys out here," I hollered. There was a nice solid wood fence around the backyard. They came outside looking very sheepish wearing those pink panties. I handed Aaron the water hose. "Get to work, sports."

Soon they were as wet as the car. It was a delight to see those cocks through the thin fabric of those panties. I watched as they squirted and chased each other with the hose. They stumbled and fell into the water and came out with suds all in their hair. The panties slid down their thighs and they stood bare ass naked drying off the car. They had to frequently bend and stoop, so I got a good look at the deep brown eye staring from the middle of those asses. A small puddle of mud formed in the yard. So, what did they do? They frolicked in the mud.

"You will not come in this House all covered with mud, young men." I'm sure I must have sounded just like my dear old Mother. I grabbed the water hose and hosed them down prison style, making them spread those ass cheeks much to their delight. I grabbed some towels and they dried themselves thoroughly on the back porch.

Soon we were all snuggled in bed for a nice afternoon nap. Juan's ass cheeks pressed against my belly and Aaron's cock rested against my back.

Dress Up

Thank goodness this house has two stories. The boys can be upstairs out of my hair while I chill downstairs on the couch knitting. Mother taught me how and it's a great way to calm nerves. Believe me when you have two rambunctious urchins in your house, you're going to either knit or drink. So, I'm sitting downstairs in the living room in my own world when I hear a lot of activity upstairs. I didn't pay much attention at first. But I heard a familiar squeak. It sounded like Mother's closet door. She refused to oil the hinges. The squeak was kind of an alarm to alert her if anyone was going in there to bother her cute nighties—namely me. So, I sat for a moment and noticed the pitter-patter of feet was definitely coming from her room and not the boy's room. I got up and tiptoed upstairs.

"You look good, bitch!" I heard Aaron squeal as Juan paraded around mom's room. He had on one of her short red negligees trimmed in a feathery white boa.

"You too, girl!" Juan shot back to Aaron rocking a black see-through teddy.

Mother's bed was littered with her naughty nighties and stiletto slippers.

"What the hell is going on here?" I was furious.

"Aw we're just having a little fun, Ed"

"Yeah. Why were you keeping all this cool stuff from us?"

"That's not 'cool stuff.' Those are my dearly departed mom's nightwear."

"Wow she was cool. All my grandma wore around the house were t-shirts and flannel pajama bottoms," Aaron sighed as he admired himself in the mirror.

"If you were skinny like us, you could wear these around the house." Juan said examining a pair of Mom's blue silk panties.

"You have no right to be in here violating my dead Mother's shrine!"

30

"What you gonna do? Spank us again?"

"Exactly!"

"You gotta catch us first." And with that, Juan and Aaron took off running around the room. I bolted after them. I never thought I'd ever be chasing anyone wearing silky negligees. I've chased after asses in silk boxers before, but never teddies and panties. Watching Juan's and Aaron's sweet little cakes bouncing in front of me soon had my cock bulging and ready for attention.

I caught Juan first when he tripped over one of Mother's stiletto heels. He fell across the bed. I jumped on top and straddled him. I wrestled him across my knees and went to work on his ass with my hand. What a sight we made reflected in the mirror. Juan's ankles and legs kicked the air while I slapped that ass as hard as I could.

"Stand up!" I commanded. I made him pull off the silk top and put him across my knees for some more punishment. There's nothing sexier and hotter than spanking a cute young man wearing red silk panties. However, I thought my message would be more effective if that ass was bare. I pulled the panties down just below his ass cheeks. His ass was almost as red as the panties. However, his squirming and giggling told me he needed a few more swats.

In the meantime, Aaron stood in the hall peeking through the door at me heating up Juan's ass. He wore Mom's blue baby doll pajamas. I could see by the way his cock strained against the blue silky panties; he was enjoying the sight of me spanking Juan's ass.

"Look at Daddy spanking Juan's ass." He began taunting and teasing Juan while at the same time shaking his blue silk bottom in my face. I made Juan stand in the corner with the red silk panties around his knees. Then it was Aaron's turn. He gave a half attempt at running, but I knew he was only playing. He also "accidently" tripped and fell across the bed on his back. That gave me another idea besides the over-the-knee routine I had given Juan. While he was on his back, I lifted his legs up by his ankles in my large brawny hands. I slapped each cheek as hard as I could.

His dick poked through the waistband of the panties. I figured I might as well give it the freedom it deserved. I pulled the panties down his long tan legs to his ankles. I bent his knees toward his chest, which left that sweet, puckered asshole exposed. I began to slap those butt cheeks. He looked so cute squirming and pretending I was hurting him. Sometimes I let my hand "slip" and whacked that juicy hole. He yelped more in delight than pain. His cock bulged and pulsated. Little pearls of pre-cum wet the tip.

Satisfied that his bottom was nice and red as a tomato, I made him stand in the corner next to Juan. That made a nice Kodak moment. Juan stood in red panties around his knees and Aaron with only a silky baby-doll top. However, watching the young men giggling and pinching each other, told me more punishment was necessary. I made Juan pull off those panties. I made both boys bend over and stand with their legs spread as wide as possible. I retrieved Grandpa's old leather strap. I made them jack their dicks while I inflicted light strokes across each bare bottom. I was soon overcome with excitement, and I had to pull out my own meat. What a delectable sight in the old wall mirror of balls bouncing as they pumped and jacked. As they were about to come, I made them face each other. I didn't want that cum all over the floor of Dear Mom's room. They jacked and came on each other's belly. They took turns licking each other clean. Of course, they eagerly kneeled on the floor in front of me. I had two eager mouths ready to receive some nice juicy come.

After that punishment, they came to my bed. Juan carried a huge jar of Vaseline. Both boys complained that their cakes were sore. It was a delight to rub those two bare red asses until they fell asleep.

Breakfast in Bed

Alas another year and another ring on the ol' tree here. Yes it was my birthday. As a treat, Aaron and Juan decided to make me pancakes and sausage and serve me in bed. Of course, I had to sneak and peep at them in the kitchen. There they worked, butt naked feverishly scrambling eggs and whipping up pancake batter. Now this scene would have raised the blood pressure of any health inspector. Of course, boys being boys, they just had to play. Juan decided it would be cute to stick a smoked sausage up Aaron's ass. Well, I guess Aaron thought it was cute too, because he waddled around the kitchen quacking like a duck with the sausage sticking halfway out his ass. I tipped back to my room before they spotted me. I could only imagine what special sauce went into the pancake batter.

Fifteen minutes later the boys came into my room bearing two silver trays with their breakfast and mine. Of course, they wore their birthday suits just like they had worn in the kitchen. Plates were piled high with pancakes dripping with syrup.

"Happy Birthday, Ed," they chimed. We piled into bed making a mess eating pancakes as the syrup dripped all over us. I picked up my sausage and took a whiff of it before biting into it. Juan and Aaron looked at each other and giggled.

"Why did you do that, Ed?" Juan teased.

"I always sniff my food before I eat it."

"Well, if it smells bad, blame it on his ass." Juan pointed at Aaron.

"Bitch my ass stays clean."

"Whore, you got more croutons up your ass than a salad bar."

"Ed, whose ass do you think is the cleanest?" Both boys lifted their knees back and showed me their holes.

"There's only one way to find out," I said. I picked up two sausages and jabbed them into each asshole. They yelped in surprised delight. When I pulled out the sausage, I took a bite of each one. "Hmm, still not sure." I got one my knees and pulled both of them close together. I drove my tongue into Juan's pink hole first. He wiggled as I pushed deeper. I left his hole and went for Aaron's darker puckered asshole. It was rougher and my tongue traveled over the soft puckering ridges. Both boys grabbed a sausage from the plate and began driving them into their asses along with my flickering tongue. They stroked their cocks as I reached up and played with their nipples.

Just as they began to moan, I slapped their hands from their cocks. I grabbed the bottle of maple syrup and drenched each dick with a generous helping of sticky sweetness. I plunged down first on Aaron's curved banana. In the meantime, I kept my hand lightly stroking Juan. Lord, if all buffets were this much fun!

It took only a moment, but hot salty boy juice began to erupt from those cocks. I filled my mouth with warm milk from each gushing faucet. That was the best breakfast I ever had. IHOP doesn't come close.

Brutus Meets The Boys

"What do ya mean, get cleaned up," Juan asked as he scratched his big balls through the opening in his boxers. He held his fingers out to Aaron who licked them.

"We are going to have dinner guests. I want you two and this place nice and clean," I said ducking Juan's ball smelling fingers.

"Somebody is coming here for real?" Aaron asked as if I had announced the Pope was coming.

"Yes someone is coming here," I sneered. "My good friend Brutus is coming to dinner."

"Brutus? Is he a dog?"

"Brutus is a man."

"Is he hot? Does he have a big cock?"

"None of that concerns you. Just go hop in the shower while I straighten up and get dinner on the stove."

"Can we help you clean up? I can dust."

"I love pushing that big ass Big Bertha around," Aaron said referring to my mother's old vacuum. For some reason twinks seem fascinated by the roaring pink and white beast. I think it's the noise.

"Yes Aaron, you can push Big Bertha. And you can dust, Juan. Let me get you some rags."

"I don't need any rags, Ed. These old boxers make a nice dust rag. My ma used my pops old drawers to clean the house."

Juan whipped off his undies and commenced to dusting a large, framed portrait of Dear Old Mother. Rest her soul, I'm sure she never had any undies waved in her face like that. Of course, it was a nice sight for me too seeing that big cock of his swinging and swaying as he went about dusting. Aaron didn't want to feel left out. He promptly stripped out of his drawers too. I watched his bronze ass quiver and strain as he pushed the vacuum. The sight of all that made me almost forget to put dinner on. I had some idea what to serve for dessert.

****

Juan and Aaron sat mesmerized watching Brutus shove forkfuls of spaghetti down his throat.

"You're so hot," Juan said eying Brutus' large biceps work as he ate.

"I bet you have a nice dick too. But Ed told us we had to behave during dinner."

"Ed's a big pussy," Brutus said looking at me.

"Freckles is the only pussy in this house," I said in my defense.

"Where is that bastard anyway," Brutus asked looking around.

"Safe and sound."

"Boys, did Ed tell you about the time Freckles got a finger stuck up his ass?"

"Oh my God, only Brutus would bring up that story," I thought. I tried to give him a signal to shut his mouth.

"I say, Ed, you're blinking like some cum splattered in your eye. You need a napkin?"

I sat there flustered. There was nothing anyone could do to stop Brutus's mouth once he got started on a story, unless you shoved a cock in it. He was the least favorite of Mother's when I invited gusts to dinner.

"Yep, boys, Ed and I threw an orgy party right there in the room you sleep in."

"An orgy party in this mausoleum?" Juan piped up.

"Don't let that pussy face fool you, fellas."

"Ed you said we couldn't have a party," Aaron pouted.

"Well, if y'all do have a party, keep that damned cat locked up somewhere. Unless he wants a finger up his ass again."

Well, you know how cats are. They like to lie on their backs with their legs in the air. I didn't even know Freckles had slipped into the room. A cat being a cat always gets in the way of your busiest activity. For instance, writing. The tapping of keys must be some kind of music. Here they come meowing and trying to rub their heads against the keyboard.

So anyway, I suppose a "guest" mistook Freckles furry belly for our Friend Bill's furry ass. Just imagine a bear, and you have a mental picture of Bill's ass. The next thing we heard was a blood curdling scream and a loud hiss. Of course, Freckles had his claws extended as he bounded over naked backs and asses in his get-away—which caused a lot more screaming and yelping.

Brutus sat at the table laughing and lapping at his mouth with his tongue like a man who just slurped a bucket load of cum. "What's for fucking dessert around here? Gawd, I'm going to miss your mom's apple pie. You should have kept the old broad on a ventilator around here just so she could make pies."

"Show us your cock and we'll be dessert," Juan chimed in.

"Gentlemen, we will not have those kinds of activities at the dinner table."

"Let's go in the living room and crash on that big ol' couch while Mother Hen here washes the dishes. By the way your spaghetti was delicious as always. I love those cock size weinies you add with those spicy meatballs." Brutus licked his big red lips and belched.

Juan and Aaron followed Brutus into the living room while I cleared the table. In a moment squealing laughter rolled down the hall towards me. I finished up in the kitchen and tipped into the living room. There stood Brutus with his pants down by his ankles while Aaron and Juan examined his twelve-inch cock. Yep, they don't call him Brutus for nothing. Even Mother's framed picture on the fireplace mantle had a quizzical expression. The boys examined Brutus' cock with all the attention a paleontologist gives a dinosaur bone. They picked it up by the massive head and ran their fingers up and down the veiny shaft. They sniffed it and measured with their hands. Juan brushed by me and ran upstairs. He came back with Mother's sewing measuring tape. He measured Brutus' cock from the head to the base from which the big balls hung like rocks. Then they measured the circumference. The measuring tape was as round as a small saucer. Juan then dropped to his knees and opened his mouth. He stretched as far as he could, but there was no way for him to get that thing past his lips. Aaron helped by grabbing Juan's upper and lower jaw and pulling them apart like someone pulling apart an alligator's mouth. Brutus' cock slid in, and Juan's lips clamped around it air-tight. Aaron had to pull it apart again. Brutus started to rock back and forth then faster until he started punishing Juan's tonsils. Imagine a small fish caught on a lure big enough to catch a whale. Aaron massaged Brutus' balls.

"C' mon, Ed, come join the fun," Brutus yelled.

I declined. Having a roll of salami shoved down my throat is not my idea of fun. Juan however, seemed up to be enjoying himself with much pleasure. His jaws were crimson and puffed out like a frog's. He started to heave and turn blue. Suddenly he pushed himself off Brutus' cock and let out a loud "Gaaaaaaag" as his gut dry heaved.

"Wow, girl, you worked that dick as best you could." Aaron patted Juan's shoulder as if his buddy had lost some kind of epic race. "But a dick like that needs an ass."

"Aw nah, girl, don't you do that." Juan knew what Aaron had in mind. Aaron promptly ignored his friend.

"Come on, Brutus lie down on the couch."

They stripped Brutus of his boots and jeans. Aaron slipped out of his jeans and bikini briefs. He spat on Brutus' cock and hoisted himself over Brutus' belly.

"Whoa, Nelly!" Brutus cried out. "I don't think spit going to be the ticket unless your ass is a twat that just birthed a baby."

"Hold on, guys," Juan shouted as he ran by me and bounded up the stairs. While he was gone, Aaron grabbed and teased Brutus' cockhead against his asshole. I saw his hole quivering and puckering with anticipation. Juan returned with a bucket-sized jar of Elbow Grease. There should be a warning on that jar: NOT FOR COCKS OVER NINE INCHES. But who would pay that any attention? Juan lathered

Brutus's cock generously until it glistened. He slapped a generous amount across Aaron's asshole. Then Aaron went to work.

Birthing a baby is often described as the miracle of life. If you ask me, birthing a twelve-inch cock up your ass is a miracle in stupidity. But boys being boys.

"Arrgh! Mother of Mercy!" Aaron shouted out as he descended over the cock. Juan stroked his arm as one might stroke a young mother giving birth for the first time. "Jesus!"

I personally didn't think the Lord was going to intervene, so I spoke up. "Aaron, perhaps you and Juan would have more fun playing with one of those nice cucumbers from the vegetable crisper." By this time Aaron was sweating like a pig at a barbecue.

"I can do this, Wilbur. I can do this," he said like one resigned to martyrdom. Juan of course consoled him with all the sincerity of the Virgin Mary at the cross of Jesus.

"Arrghh! More Elbow Grease! More Elbow Grease!" Juan obeyed with another generous helping. "Eeeyyaaah!"

"Okay, that's enough." I walked over to Aaron and pulled him up from Brutus' cock. A fart rushed out long and mournful as if going on a long journey. Of course, there was much protesting and calling me a "wussy pussy." But in the end, Daddy knows best. I will not be explaining to the Doctor in an emergency room why a twink's ass looks like a truck ran up in it. Brutus gave them a nice parting gift of a couple of generous facials, which they greedily licked off each other.

"This is much better than some ol' lady's pie," Juan said between licks.

"Indeed, it is," Brutus said as he licked the two assholes sitting an inch from his face.

The Onesie Wardrobe Malfunction

"Boo!"

I opened one eye. I wondered why in the hell a pair of Teletubbies stood by the couch? Or was that Winnie the Pooh and Tigger?

"How do you like them?" Juan and Aaron asked in unison.

Before I could answer, they turned around and unzipped the back flaps. They bent over shaking their cute round asses at me.

"We bought these for our party," Juan said.

"Um hello fellas, but normally people don't bother buying anything special to wear to an orgy."

"It's not just an orgy. It's going to be a onesies pajama jam," said Aaron.

"Yeah. Guys can't wear nothing to the party but onesies."

"With nothing underneath."

"Whether they come by car, or bus—just onesies and no draws underneath."

"Those things are hideous," I hissed.

"There's that old guy thinking again. Well at least Brutus is coming."

"Yeah, he's going to wear a fucking jockstrap! Imagine driving ten miles in a convertible just wearing a jock," Aaron swooned.

"I'm sure the cops can't imagine it," I said.

"I wonder if they got one big enough for that cock of his?"

"Men at his age often wear diapers."

"Stop hating, Ed."

"I want to hold it in my mouth again," Juan said licking his lips.

"Girl, you worked that dick."

"I been training since I was six years old. I grew up with a bunch of nasty boy cousins."

"All I had was girl cousins. I'm glad they didn't make me lick their kitties," Aaron said.

"Well enough of all of that, guys."

"Is Brutus going to bring his whip? I want to see some asses get beat red as apples."

"It's only a prop."

"Aw. You probably won't let him."

"Believe me, I'd welcome him to tan a couple of asses around here."

"Whose?"

"Never mind. You need to help get this pigsty cleaned up, if you're going to throw a party."

"Let's polish the banisters in our onesies!"

They bounded up the stairs and slid down several times. At the top of the stairs, the banister has a broken off knob. A screw with the sharp end exposed sticks up. I've been meaning to get it fixed for months. Normally it's not a problem, because anyone can see the screw and simply avoid touching it. And I never expected to see anyone's ass slide down the stairs.

"Yow!"

I jumped off the couch and ran to the hall. There hung Aaron suspended from the fabric of his onesie with his head about two feet from the floor. He had been trying to beat Juan to the first floor and decided to leap over the railing and got his bottoms caught on the screw. There he was suspended in mid-air with his tush all nice, round, and exposed like the full moon. Juan of course was laughing his ass off. Aaron didn't find it funny at all. He flailed his arms and squawked to get let out of his trap. I came up with an idea to help him find humor in his situation. Since the boys enjoyed playing in Mother's negligees and feathery boas, I had just the ticket. I went to her room and found a long peacock feather.

I caressed Aaron around his ears to give him the sensation of a gnat flying and lighting on them. He swatted and smacked his face until it was hot pink. I then moved to his ass. He tried to swat at his ass and the feather, but his hands couldn't reach up above his back. I stroked the area between his balls and asshole.

"Stop Ed, stop!" He began to giggle. I had put an ottoman under his head in case more of the fabric gave way and sent him crashing to the floor. What a sight it was to see that tush wiggling trying to get away from the feathery torture. His laughter filled the house like that of a braying mule as I tickled him unmercifully for about an hour. What a Marquis de Sade I can be sometimes. Juan didn't want to be left out of the fun and unzipped the ass flap of his onesie. I gave his ass a few hard slaps and sent him to the corner to play in his milk and cookies.

I returned to tickling Aaron's ass and inner thighs. I would have gone for his feet, but they were covered with the padded sole of the onesie.

"Haaaw! Huhh! Haaaw! Huyuck!" His laughter left him gasping for air and speechless.

After a moment, Aaron's onesie mercifully ripped and sent him crashing into the ottoman. I smacked his ass and sent him to stand in the corner next to Juan. What a sight—two nice round asses red as apples standing in the corner in torn onesies. After that, the onesie party idea vanished.

The Twinkies and Milk Soiree

Or Ride That Pony

"Suck those cocks now!"

Brutus stood butt naked in the middle of a mound of quivering asses. I swear the entire United Nations was represented. Cute little black asses, nice round brown asses, large black cocks curving right and left. Uncut young Arabic cocks with rolls of foreskin disappeared into hungry mouths. Tan and white cakes that made your hand want to slap them bounced around the room. Balls jiggled and bobbed. A twink wore Brutus' Jockstrap on his head like a crown. Brutus cracked his whip in the air and shouted commands like the captain of a Viking ship. It sounded like a hog pen as hungry mouths went after cocks and assholes. Two boys hung onto Brutus' thighs and eagerly ran their tongues up and down his cock-shaft. One tried to swallow Brutus's cock, but fearing he would get lockjaw, he gave up. What added life to the party was Brutus' portable sling get-up he had fashioned out of one of those rocky horse things on springs. In fact Brutus left the head on but had the horse's body cut away. Instead of a horse's plastic rump, there was a wide strap of leather to hold your ass. To make it strong enough to hold adults, he had added shock absorbers from a Honda Civic. You were reared back and had to hold onto the reins to keep from falling to the floor. The boys put their feet in the stirrups leaving their ass for all to explore. And what an exploration it was. Cucumbers that I had been saving for salad wound up stuck in quite a few buttholes—quite gleefully. Cocks pointed straight up in the air as twinks rode the sling.

Brutus stood in front of the sling, swinging it back and forth—his cock head gently brushing and teasing assholes. I had been relegated to answering the door and serving refreshments which included lemonade punch laced with cheap vodka. All of the twinks were over the age of eighteen. I felt if they were fit for war and fucking, why not a little taste of something strong in the punch. I had also been explicitly warned not to let any fat boys into the party.

"Suck those assholes, you young fuckers!"

Brutus was certainly taking charge of things. Knees bent back near to ears. I had never seen so many cute brown eyes winking and puckering. If someone had dusted them with glitter, those assholes would have put the solar system to shame. Tongues slurped as they rooted deeply in search of buried treasure.

Brutus' cock became the life of the party as the alcohol flowed and loosened those inhibitions and let loose that young man bravado. Generous amounts of *Elbow Grease* were applied to cock and ass—and a few lips. But fearing permanent injury to the rectum or lockjaw they gave up. They resigned themselves to pouring lemonade on it and licking it like a popsicle. A twelve-inch cock is a lovely novelty to behold, but not many ass champions can rise to that challenge. Most of Brutus' sex life revolved around inflatable dolls, or being on display like he was that night. Don't tell him I said so.

"I want to see some cocks shoved up some asses!" Brutus cracked his whip loudly. "If you're not paired off, you have to come to daddy for a spanking!" Quickly bottoms went up in the air and dicks drove in. I loved hearing that "Shlock Shlock" as those dicks went in and out. The odd number boy had no choice but to lie across Brutus' lap and receive a nice daddy spanking. Judging by the way his legs kicked at the air, I think he thoroughly enjoyed it.

It was getting late past three a.m. Brutus and those twinks were nowhere near exhausted. He had brought some ropes and was demonstrating the art of tying knots around ankles and hands. Just imagine your thanksgiving turkey all trussed up. That's how the twinks looked to me. Still, I was getting tired. The sights and sounds of all that fucking was enough to wear me out. Plus, Dean Wolf was going to stop by in the morning to check on the boys. I certainly didn't want him to see boys stumbling out of the front door half naked or a mound of flesh passed out in the living room. I had hinted and harrumphed several times at Brutus, but he promptly ignored me when a pair of lips sought out his cock.

The doorbell rang. It was four a.m. I wondered who the devil that could be. I opened the door with every intention to shoo whoever it was away. Now fellas, there is skinny-fat and fat-fat. Most of us Daddies are skinny-fat. We've got a gut just hanging a tad bit over the belt. We may still have nice legs and nice shaped asses. But fat-fat is the Pillsbury Doughboy twice over. I mean this kid was huge. He sort of just rolled in through the door. I shrugged and showed him where to undress. The twinks were too buzzed and busy with cocks to notice right away. I began counting down the minutes for him to emerge from the bathroom. If that fat ass couldn't gross out the twinks and send them home, nothing could.

Now when I say rolls, I'm not talking about little bitty dinner rolls. I mean rolls of something you might buy in bulk like carpet or hog hides. The tits on that boy had to be as big as a country girl hookers. His stomach touched the middle of his thighs. He was as white, and cellulite dimpled as cottage cheese. Smelled like it too. When he waddled into the party room, Mouths stopped sucking in mid-dick. Dicks deflated in asses. Even Brutus's dick got shy and shrunk to ten inches.

"Whee! Whee!" The fat boy lifted his belly and jiggled his cock. Well, I think it was a cock. It might have been a baby's thumb. He shook and shimmied like three tubs of jello at a jello wrestling match. He got down and crawled on all fours and rooted like a warthog. I had not expected any kind of performance like this. But I remembered smelling some alcohol on his breath. I assumed he was drunk. Suddenly he got up and bellowed like a bull. He then bent low and using his fingers as horns ran toward a group of twinks. They scattered out of the way like chickens. He plowed straight into Brutus' ass. I heard Brutus let go a loud fart and his dentures flew out of his mouth. The party was over.

"Goodnight," I said to each twink stumbling out of the house trying to get into their pants.

I learned later that fatboy had been hired to entertain as a stripper at a party down the street. He had gotten the addresses mixed up. Juan and Aaron didn't speak to me for a couple of days. It was bliss around the house for a moment.

Halloween Payback

"I'm going to be a caveman."

"Bitch, you wear that tired ass costume every Halloween."

"But this time, I'm going to wear heels." Juan produced a pair of my mother's old stilettos.

"Who ever heard of a caveman in heels?"

"It's called creativity. It's much better than your Nun-slut outfit of black kimono top and nun's veil."

"Boys like my legs."

"They like what's between them."

"I once went dressed as Superman," I said trying to get in on the fun.

"Everyone does Superman. That's so lame. Now Lois Lane, that's another story. Punks should dress as Lois Lane." Juan and Aaron high-fived each other.

Since the boys enjoyed playing dress-up so much, I thought I'd get in one the act also. Their time would soon be up at my home. Dean Wolf had informed us that the male dorms were days away from being ready. I decided the boys should have a nice memory to last them for the rest of their lives. I had squirreled away one of mom's silk bathrobes and her frizzy wig. I waited patiently until I heard the water running in the upstairs shower. I knew they'd be getting ready to go out to *Club Boyland* for an evening of Halloween fun. I dressed in the robe and wig and picked up the rubber dagger along with a fake blood pack I had gotten from a costume shop. I secreted the fake blood capsule in my left hand. I tipped slowly up the stairs. The bathroom door was ajar and little curls of steam drifted out of the room. Water blasted hard in the shower. I could barely make out their asses wiggling and pressed against the shower door. I raised my hand that held the knife and readied the blood to squirt. I pushed open the door. Aaron saw me first and started to laugh. As Juan turned around, I lunged at him with the fake dagger and squirted the blood onto his chest at the same time. He screamed in

47

surprise. Aaron saw the fake blood. Thinking Juan had been stabbed, He screamed louder and covered his dick. I lunged and slashed at Juan with the dagger. Each time I lunged I squirted more blood. I gave Aaron a few whacks with the dagger on his shoulders. He and Aaron thought for certain they were being stabbed to death. They had no idea the blade was as limp as an old man's cock. They tried to make a break for the narrow shower door opening. I body blocked them. Of course, some of the fake blood got on the robe. They assumed it was theirs. They began to scream for help. Red suds filled the shower. That added to their panic, and they hollered like crazy.

I slipped on a wet tile and the boys bolted by me. I recovered my footing and took off behind them. They yelled and screamed bloody murder as they ran down the stairs toward the front door. One of them stepped on Freckle's tail. The blood-curdling yowl he uttered added to their panic. They got to the front door and twisted the knob. Their hands were wet and slippery and couldn't get a firm grip. They tried the deadbolt, but I had removed the key. They banged on the door with their fists and kicked it. What a sight they were, naked hugging, trembling and pissing on the floor as I approached with the knife raised above my head. About three feet away, I whipped out my phone and took a nice picture before rolling on the floor with laughter. Needless to say, they were not too happy to be scared piss-less. But I was a happy camper as I rolled on the floor delirious with laughter and soaking up their piss.

"Fucker!" Juan yelled as he and Aaron slammed the bathroom door to finish their shower.

Goodbye

The college finally got the dorms ready. Dean Wolf seemed delighted to break the news to me. Greedy bastard. He wants all of those twinks for himself. He likes to make unannounced early inspections of the male dorms. He says he's looking for liquor or other forbidden contraband. But I know it's all about those erect morning cocks. Me and the boys asked Wolf if we could continue to stay together? But he cited some silly rule that said all freshmen must live on campus. Plus there would be no more stipend money. Yeah right, I thought. However, he did consent and let them spend the last weekend with me, if I promised to drive the boys to school Monday morning.

"We sure hate to go. We've had so much fun," Aaron said as he leaned in between my legs and stroked my balls. It was Sunday night and we lounged in Mother's big old brass four-poster bed.

"Yeah," Juan agreed. He flicked a feather across my hard nipples.

"Maybe we should drop out of college. I could stay here and suck this cock every day," Aaron grinned up at me.

"Me too," said Juan.

Although the prospect was nice, I don't think I could take months of those two rambunctious young men. Six weeks was enough.

"You know Ed, we never got a chance to fuck you," Aaron said.

"Yeah," Juan agreed. He took a puff from his joint. "I've always wanted to fuck a daddy type."

Yes I did allow the boys to have the liberty of smoking a joint or two. It seemed to keep them calm and horny at the same time.

"Now listen up, boys, I'm the Daddy of the house. You're ..."

"Look what we found in your Dear old Mother's closet," Juan said. He held up a blue dildo the size of a large cucumber. I nearly lost my breath. No wonder my dear old Mom never married after pops died. Where would she find a man like that?

"This will be more fun than fucking you," Juan said. "Fucking is a lot of work."

"You're just a bottom bitch anyway," Aaron teased.

"Bitch, the Doctor can see your brains from your cootchie. They named the Panama Canal after you."

"Boys, the Panama Canal was built in the early 1900's."

"They knew that bitch was coming," Juan pointed at Aaron.

Juan lay on my right and Aaron lay on my left side. They both stroked my shoulders, chest, and nipples. Aaron reached down and stroked my cock. Juan kept the action going around my nipples. Soon my legs were parted enough for Juan to stroke my balls while Aaron nibbled on my earlobes and neck. His tongue flickered across my lips. I parted my mouth and his tongue brushed across the tip of my tongue and lips. Now most young twinks limit themselves to giving you a good cock sucking at most. But soft lips and a sweet tongue flickering over yours is heaven-sent to say the least.

Juan was doing such a good job with my balls, my thighs parted easily to allow him access. He sucked my cock and balls. There's no sweeter sight or feeling than seeing a ring of curls and a pair of sweet lips giving your cock and balls the royal treatment. Juan left my cock and joined Aaron in the kissing game. Now I had two sweet tongues and two pairs of lips sending shivers down my spine. We sucked each other's tongues and mopped each other's lips.

The boys turned their attention to the dildo and began kissing and sucking the massive play toy. They reminded me of sucking big blue popsicles on a hot summer day. Only their lips weren't blue. Juan being the more daring placed the dildo as far in his mouth as humanly possible—in fact a little too far. He had started to turn blue and wave his arms before I reached up and yanked the darn thing out of his mouth.

"See, there are some challenges even too great for you," I said as he wheezed and caught his breath. Of course, Aaron thought it was hilarious.

Once Juan regained his composure and with that dildo thoroughly wet, Aaron and Juan lifted my legs, kept them bent at the knees and spread them wide apart. That left my manhole exposed and vulnerable to the machinations of those mischievous young bucks. Aaron worked the dildo around my asshole. I moaned with pleasure and would have been quite satisfied with that. Juan spread my hole with his fingers and Aaron aimed right for the dead center. He pushed and pulled with each push deeper than the next one.

"Wow, you know what would be hot?" Juan grasped Aaron's hand and made him stop.

I don't know about you, but once a train starts to enter a tunnel on its journey, you don't want to stop nor back it up. The only way through a tunnel is all the way through it. So there I was lying there like a whore on the gynecologist table while they discussed what would be hot.

"What, we try to stick Freckles up his ass?" said Aaron.

"No Silly. Remember when Wilbur scared us like in that movie Psycho?"

"Ed!" I yelled.

"Yeah, that wasn't nice, Ed Wilbur," Aaron said. He twisted the dildo to mark his displeasure.

"Ow!" I yelped.

"Let's get that wig and put it on him. And let's videotape it."

"Cool man. Let's call it 'Sex-o Psycho.'"

Aaron and Juan leaped off the bed and ran towards Mother's room. They left me with my legs up and Mother's dildo firmly planted in my ass. I would have tried to pull it out, but my hands were bound to the bed with a pair of dear old mom's pantyhose. Yes, I had forgotten that little detail.

Soon they came running back into the room with the frizzy wig.

"Now boys if you think I'm going to lie here and let you put that wig on me..."

"You had your fun, now it's our turn."

"I wish we had something to stuff in his mouth."

"We do." Juan straddled my chest and stuck his hard cock in my mouth. Aaron arranged the wig on my head and set up his digital camera on some books on the dresser so that it aimed right at the bed.

"Action!" He yelled and he leaped into the bed and continued driving the dildo toward the tunnel of my ass. Juan worked my mouth and tonsils with his cock. I closed my eyes. Suddenly, I saw her coming. She had the hot water bottle in her hand. There was a syringe attached to a hose. I had been constipated for almost a week after sneaking into the Christmas basket and eating a bit of every cheese sample I could find. My tummy was swollen to the size of a little round cake. She told me to get out of my pants and undies and crawl up into her bed. Mother laid a towel under my bottom. "Just in case," she said as she rubbed the end of the syringe with Vaseline.

"This won't hurt, Edward. Not at all."

To make sure, she dabbed some of the Vaseline around my anus. Then she slowly inserted the syringe inside me. She released the clamp and warm water flowed and filled my belly. She felt my stomach and it was tight as a drum. She shut off the clamp and stopped the water.

"Let's try to go, Edward."

Mother led me to the bathroom and sat me on the commode. I unclenched my ass hole and let loose all of that cheese—all of it. She flushed the toilet twice. When I was finished, she gave me a bath and put me in the bed next to her.

My eyes popped open just in time for me to see Juan's cum aiming at my face. My own cum exploded against my chest. I lay there for a moment after they untied me. I felt Aaron pull the dildo out of my ass. I grabbed his hand and made him stop. I wanted that moment and that memory to last forever.

Later that night Juan and Aaron watched the video and debated which online site would pay the most money for "Sex-o Psycho." I thought only of Mother.

###

Epilogue

Boy Talk

The First Time

It was sweet, sweet as a Popsicle
My first cock was, sweet and big
As a pickle in a five gallon jar
Sitting on a bodega counter
In Harlem.
It was juicy
Juicy as an orange in summer
It was full of blood and ill-mannered,
Pushing my protesting tongue
Out of the way, the way
Your big brothers elbow you
From the last biscuit.
It was wrapped in dollar bills
And smoke blazing towards
A dusty ceiling fan.
I wanted it because
That dimpled chin,
Soft plum-flavored lips,
And them dime colored eyes
Told me it would be something good.
It was.

#################

Mine was black and sour
As old buttermilk
It pointed rudely to the right
Like a bat aiming at a skull

It was ugly and full of veins
I wanted to bite it
But the knife's blade
Glared in my eyes.
I obeyed the man
Who beat my Mother.
I endured his names
Of punk and faggot, uttered
Even as he choked me
On his cock.
I did it as he sat on the commode
His favorite seat in the house
His turds floated beneath my chin.
My life was no crystal stair.
I ran away at sixteen
He brought me back
And roped me to the
Chinaberry tree
behind the high fence.
He turned on his boom-box
And dashed the remains of
His forty-ounce on my wounds
And called for my mama
To bring him another
And another and another
This dragon tattoo
Breathing fire down my back
Hides his malice,
But my wounds run deep
As I suck cock after cock
for bread and muscular arms.

Charles Harvey

About the Author

AC Adams loves gay erotica and wants you to love it also. That's why he's always striving to give you a lot of bang for your buck, so you can bang your buck. Someone said the best way for a young man to earn a living is to write about what he loves. I've taken writing courses at the University level and online through workshops. Courses alone don't make one a better writer. A keen eye for detail and a lot of heart have to be added to the mix.

At the heart of my writing are my experiences. I'm a fiction writer not a memoirist. I fictionalize my truth and the truth of others.

I learned the craft of creative expression from my Mother. She taught me in more ways than one how to make up stories and to give people we knew alternate lives. I'm a member of Erotic Meets, the premier group for Erotica Writers. My unofficial Birth date is August 19, 1987. I'm not much younger or older than that. I've adopted Texas right now. The kindness of readers keeps me going.

Follow AC

https://twitter.com/ACAdams1
https://www.amazon.com/author/acadams

◈ Soft Erotica – Where Heat Meets Heart

Late-night stories for grown folks.

◈ charlesharveyauthor.wordpress.com/sizzle/[1]

****

---

1.   https://charlesharveyauthor.wordpress.com/sizzle/

AC ADAMS

****

Don't miss out!

Visit the website below and you can sign up to receive emails whenever AC Adams publishes a new book. There's no charge and no obligation.

https://books2read.com/r/B-A-MKYB-NQOG

BOOKS 2 READ

Connecting independent readers to independent writers.

Did you love *Dorm Daddy at Home*? Then you should read *A Foursome Plus Poems*[2] by Charles Harvey and AC Adams!

Dive into 'A Foursome plus Poems', where the lines between pleasure and peril blur in a tantalizing dance. This collection isn't just stories. The poetry included takes an unapologetic plunge into the depths of gay fantasy, dripping with eroticism and shadowed by the macabre.

These narratives are a feast for the senses, where the ordinary morphs into comedic darkness. Every crunch of a crab whispers untold stories of passion. Where was that banana before it wound up in the pudding? Are cucumbers just for salad? As you traverse these pages, expect to be both charmed and unsettled, your fantasies entwined with a thread of darkness. You'll find yourself ensnared in their allure. Each story in

---

2. https://books2read.com/u/bz6OJj

3. https://books2read.com/u/bz6OJj

this collection is a foray into the depths of fantasy, where the mundane becomes steamy, and every page turns with anticipation.

Excerpt:

Banana Pudding

I peered through the window after the doorbell gonged and wondered why my gentleman caller was wearing a yellow raincoat. The sky was brilliantly blue, and the sun shined so hard the flowers in my neighbor's yard looked like plastic pinwheels. Reluctantly, I opened the door.

"I hadn't heard the weatherman say anything about rain today. I said looking him up and down."

He stood tall but bent a little at the waist. He looked at me through dark eyes that appeared like bruises in the middle of his smooth face. He hesitated as if contemplating running away. A blue bandana with the words "Chiquita Rocks" fit tight on his head. I smiled a smile that matched the sun and the yellow suit. My visitor relaxed, stamped his black boot on the welcome mat, and hopped across the threshold on one foot.

"This ain't no raincoat. It's a yellow summer coat. I like yellow."

"I see you do. It's a great color for a warm day."

"It's a great color period. You should see my friends hanging out at the grocers all green acting like young boys. They didn't believe the tree. The tree said we wouldn't be green long. The tree didn't lie. I'm a man already."

Originally Published in 2012 Revised December 2023. Poetry added

Also by AC Adams

Dorm Daddy
Dorm Daddy at Home

Kinky
The Kink Chronicles

Standalone
A Foursome
A Foursome Plus Poems

Watch for more at https://charlesharveyauthor.wordpress.com/ac-adams/.

About the Author

AC Adams loves steamy LGBTQ stories and thinks you should have the most interesting. That's why he's always striving to give you a lot of bang for your buck. Someone said the best way for a young man to earn a living is to write about what he loves. I've taken writing courses at the University level and online through workshops. Courses alone don't make one a better writer. A keen eye for detail and a lot of heart has to be added to the mix.

At the heart of my writing are my experiences. I'm a fiction writer, not a memoirist. I fictionalize my truth and the truth of others.

I learned the craft of creative expression from my mother. She taught me in more ways than one how to make up stories and to give people we knew alternate lives. My unofficial Birth date is August 19, 1987. I'm not much younger or older than that. I've adopted Texas right now. The kindness of readers keeps me going.

I realize all stories aren't for all people. But, I hope I earn my way into your heart.

Read more at https://charlesharveyauthor.wordpress.com/ac-adams/.